Retro Valentines
Kids & Animals
Grayscale Coloring Book
By Renee Davenport

Titles of Coloring Pages

1. Love My Kitty Cat
2. Sweet Heart
3. Giddy Up
4. Bowl Me Over
5. Cat in a Hat
6. Sweet Valentine
7. Roller Coaster
8. Puppy Party
9. School Daze
10. Calling all Kitties
11. Miss Chit Chat
12. Valentine for You
13. Fishing Buddies
14. Mail for You
15. Princess Bunny
16. Princess Daisy
17. Ellie
18. Chocolates for You
19. Best Buddies
20. Play Pets
21. Bake Me a Cake
22. Be Mine
23. Got You on the Line
24. Wooden Shoe
25. Bunny Love
26. Honey Bunny
27. Cowboy Heart
28. Puppy Love
29. Chasing Butterflies
30. School Girl
31. Wild About You
32. Walk in the Rain
33. Puppy on a Pillow
34. Happy Kitty

FOR YOU
ON VALENTINE'S
DAY

"WOODEN SHOE" LIKE TO BE MY VALENTINE?

BE MY HONEY BUNNY!

Thank you for coloring

Retro Valentines
Kids & Animals
Grayscale Coloring Book!

Look for more grayscale coloring books

from the series

Retro Fun

Volume 1-Fall & Winter Kids & Animals

Volume 2-Holiday Angels, Santas & Snowmen

Volume 3-Retro Valentine's Day Kids & Animals

Volume 4-Spring & Summer Kids & Animals

Plus

Four Seasons of

Retro Vintage Pin Up Girls.

Don't forget about

Sweet Girls ~ Beautiful Women,

In The Mood Retro Couples,

& the fun coloring book Airborne & Airborne Mini.

Please visit JoyfulColoringBooks.com

and join my newsletter.

Please contact me at-

JoyfulColoringBooks@gmail.com

Made in the USA
Monee, IL
08 September 2022